RHYME SLIME

WRITTEN BY ALI SPARKES

ILLUSTRATED BY SARAH HORNE

OXFORD
UNIVERSITY PRESS

OXFORD
UNIVERSITY PRESS

Great Clarendon Street, Oxford, OX2 6DP, United Kingdom

Oxford University Press is a department of the University
of Oxford. It furthers the University's objective of excellence
in research, scholarship, and education by publishing
worldwide. Oxford is a registered trade mark of Oxford
University Press in the UK and in certain other countries

Text © Ali Sparkes 2015
Illustrations © Sarah Horne 2015

The moral rights of the author have been asserted

First published 2015
This edition published 2019

British Library Cataloguing in Publication Data
Data available

ISBN: 978-0-19-276977-0

10 9 8 7 6 5 4 3 2 1

Paper used in the production of this book is a natural, recyclable product
made from wood grown in sustainable forests. The manufacturing process
conforms to the environmental regulations of the country of origin.

Printed in China

Acknowledgements
Series Advisor: Nikki Gamble

Helping your child to read

Before they start

- Talk about the back cover blurb. What does your child think might happen if you 'catch *rhyme*'?

- Look at the front cover. Does it look like a funny story or a serious story?

During reading

- Let your child read at their own pace, either silently or out loud.

- If necessary, help them to work out words they don't know by saying each sound out loud and then blending them to say the word, e.g. *s-u-dd-e-n-l-y, suddenly.*

- Encourage your child to keep checking that the text makes sense and they understand what they are reading. Remind them to re-read to check the meaning if they're not sure.

- Give them lots of praise for good reading!

After reading

- Look at page 47 for some fun activities.

Chapter One

When Jasmine woke up on Tuesday morning, she felt weird.

"I feel weird," she told her sister, Anika.

Anika snorted. "You *are* **weird**."

Jasmine suddenly said, "You've got a **beard**!"

Anika threw a pillow at Jasmine. "You look like a **bat**!"

Jasmine threw it back and said, "You smell like a **rat**."

Anika got up and stared at Jasmine. "Why are you speaking in **rhyme**?"

Jasmine said, "Why are you wasting my **time**?"

"*Dad!*" shouted Anika. "Jasmine's being weird!"

Dad came upstairs. "You have school today," he pointed out. "Jasmine, why are you still in **bed**?"
"There's something funny in my **head**," Jasmine said.

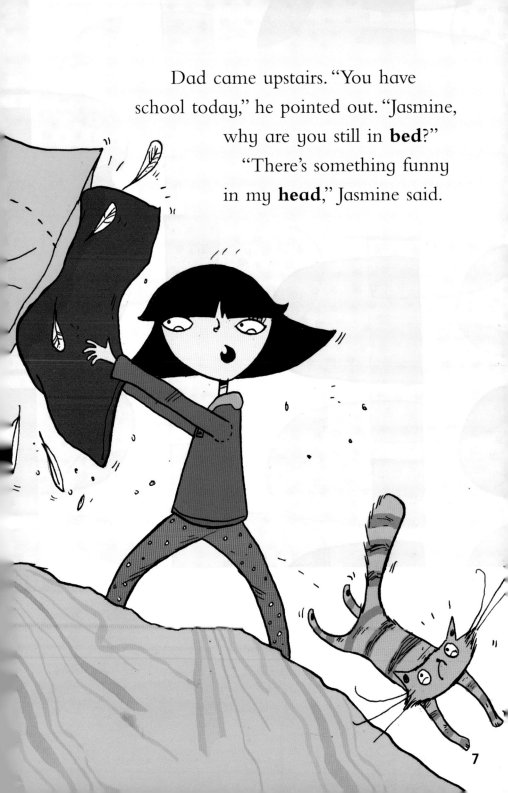

Dad touched her forehead.

"Are you feeling **hot**?"

Jasmine sighed and went cross-eyed.

"No, I'm really **not**."

Dad raised one eyebrow.
"Are you talking in **verse**?"
Jasmine said, "It's actually **worse**.

Today, I can *only* talk in **rhyme**.
Working it out takes up so much **time**.
There's a poem machine inside my **brain**!
I can't switch it off. It's a bit of a **pain**."

Dad said, "Jasmine, you're being very **silly**."
Jasmine shrugged. "Maybe it's the same for **Millie**."
"Oh, I see! It's some game you're playing with your friend," said Dad. "Well, you can talk in rhyme with Millie – but not at home. It's getting annoying. And it's time to get **dressed**."

Jasmine smiled sadly. "Am I being a **pest**?"

"I'm going downstairs," said Dad. "I've got to clean your jumper. You got some gooey green stuff on it at school yesterday. What do you *do* at that place? Get out of bed and downstairs in ten minutes. Don't make me **shout**!"

"All right!" said Jasmine. "I'm getting **out**!"

Downstairs, Jasmine found Anika and Dad prodding the green goo on her jumper. "What *is* this stuff? Your jumper's a **mess**!"

Jasmine cried, "That's IT! **Yes**! **Yes**! I didn't realise it at the **time**, but I've been infected by **Rhyme Slime**!"

Chapter Two

"What do you mean by
Rhyme Slime?" said Dad.
  Jasmine explained.

"We all went down to the park **yesterday**,
looking for tadpoles with Miss **McCray**.
Mrs Sprout, the park keeper lady, came **by**.
She stopped by the pond and let out a **cry**.
  'Oooh, don't touch that slimy stuff,
don't poke that **goo**! Haven't you heard?
You'll catch *rhyme* if you **do**!'

Although Miss McCray tried to move her **on**,
she told us all this, just before she was **gone**:
'If you dig in that pond, it'll be for the **worse**.
For you'll only be able to say things in **verse**!'"

Dad waved his hands in the air. "Are you seriously telling me that you've picked up some kind of *poem bug* … from **slime**?"

Jasmine shrugged. "It makes you **rhyme**," she said. "What Mrs Sprout said was **true**, and there's nothing at all that I can **do**."

"That is the most ridiculous thing I have *ever* heard," said Dad. "She's just pretending!" said Anika. "I'm not walking with her. She's weird." And Anika went off to school on her own.

Over breakfast, there was a huge argument. Dad said Jasmine wasn't going anywhere until she said something that didn't rhyme. They argued in poems for an hour.

Jasmine tried to convince Dad.

"Dad, I'm OK, I can still go to **school**. It's swimming! I want to go in the **pool**!"

Dad folded his arms. "Well, let's think about that, shall we? Suppose you fell in at the deep end and couldn't swim to safety. You'd want to shout '**help**'! But how would you do that if you couldn't think of a rhyme for it?"

Jasmine nodded. That would be tricky. What rhymed with 'help'?

"All I can think of," said Dad, "is **kelp**. A kind of seaweed."

"So you'd have to shout '**HELP! KELP!**'
And people would think you were being attacked
by killer seaweed. They'd think you were joking.
And by the time they realized you were in trouble …
well, it might just be too **late**."

"Then I'd be in a terrible **state**!" said Jasmine.

"Right," said Dad. "I think we should go into school and see what Miss McCray has to say about this silliness."

Chapter Three

Dad told Miss McCray about Jasmine's
endless rhyming.

"I'm sure she'll get fed up with doing this
soon," said Dad, with a sigh.

Miss McCray nodded. She didn't say anything.

As soon as Dad had gone, Miss McCray
slammed the classroom door shut and leaned
against it. She let out a long breath and then
turned to the children.

"OK, your playtime was quite **long**.

And I've had a coffee – very **strong**.

But as you can hear, I'm still speaking in **verse**.

Has anyone got any better? Or **worse**?"

21

Jasmine looked around the class in amazement.

Millie put up her hand.

"We're all still rhyming. We can't **stop it**.

No matter how we try to **drop it**."

Jasmine thought to herself,

"Everyone? They're all rhyming, **too**?

Wow! That was some powerful **goo**!"

Zack stood up.
"This is bad and it's getting **worse**!
If I can't stop talking in rhyming **verse**,
tonight when I'm out with my team on the **tracks**,
they'll be laughing so hard they'll fall flat
on their **backs**!"

Miss McCray held up her hand.
"OK, OK, let me just **say**,
I thought it would have gone **away**.
I really thought it wouldn't **last**.
Now we need some answers – **fast**."
Everyone started offering ideas.

How about we never **speak**?

We wouldn't even last a **week**!

What if we don't speak, but **sing**?

But most songs rhyme. Oh, ding-a-**ling**!

What is the cure for poem **attack**?
Some ice down your **back**?
Hop about in a **sack**?

Maybe if we eat
some **cheese**?

Or runny jam or
squishy **peas**?

What – you think
it's cured with **diet**?
Everybody!
Quiet! Quiet!

Jasmine had been very still. Now she stood up on her chair and called out, "Please be **quiet**. Let's not **riot**!"

The class fell silent.

"Listen," she said, "there might be a **way**. Who did we meet by the pond **yesterday**?"

"**Ooooooooh**," gasped everyone, as they remembered.

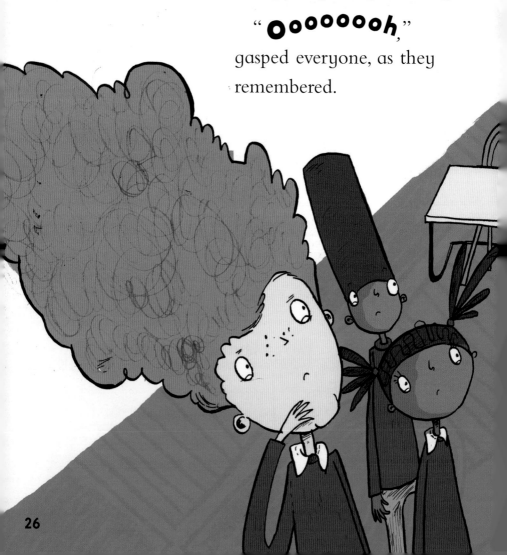

"**Goooooo!**"

they added, as they remembered even more.

Jasmine went on.

"We met the park keeper, Mrs **Sprout**,

she did tell us all we'd have to watch **out**."

Miss McCray nodded.

"I'm ashamed to say, that when Mrs **Sprout** went pink in the face and started to **shout**, I just thought she was being **dotty**. By the way, I like your book bag, **Lottie**."

Everyone blinked and Lottie looked at her book bag, which was exactly the same as everyone else's book bag. But nobody said anything. Endless rhyming was tough. If Miss McCray needed an easy rhyme that didn't make much sense, nobody blamed her.

Miss McCray kept going.
"Jasmine, you're right – Mrs **Sprout** knows what this is all **about**.
Rhyme Slime has infected us **all**.
Perhaps I'll give Mrs Sprout a **call**."

Miss McCray took her mobile phone out of her desk. A few beeps later, someone answered. Miss McCray sank into her seat.

"Oh help, Mrs Sprout, you're our only **hope**. That pond made us poets and now we can't **cope**!"

Poems!

$$4+5=?$$
$$3+3=!$$
$$7+5=$$
$$8+3$$

Mrs Sprout arrived half an hour later. By this time, everyone was outside playing sports on the field. Swimming had been called off in case anyone needed to shout '**HELP!**' but couldn't think of a rhyme.

Now they were running around the field, trying to think of words that rhymed with 'goal', 'catch' and 'tackle'. It wasn't easy. After a while, they just had to repeat the same things.

31

It was really very tiring. Soon they were not saying much at all. Well, Jade Smith, who hated all sports, was groaning, "My **legs** are **killing me**. My **eggs** are **chilling me**."

This made *no* sense – but it did rhyme perfectly.

33

Miss McCray
called everyone over.
"Come along, Class **2SB**.
Everyone, beneath the **tree**!"
They gathered under the big tree
at the corner of the playing field and
Mrs Sprout stood in front
of them, clutching a large
purple bag.
"Well!" said Mrs Sprout.
"I did try to warn you all!"

Miss McCray said,
"We're sorry we didn't believe **you**.
We just didn't think it was **true**.
For how could we all catch a poetry bug
from regular pond slime and **goo**?"

"It's Poet's Pond," said Mrs Sprout. "People have been catching verse from it for centuries. Really, Miss McCray, you ought to know your local history!"

Miss McCray looked embarrassed.

"First of all, let's see how bad it is," said Mrs Sprout. "So – anyone who answers this question will get a prize! Here goes … is my bag purple?"

There was total silence. Everyone pulled faces (some of them quite frightening) as they tried to work out a rhyme for 'purple'.

"All right then," said Mrs Sprout, digging into her purple bag. "Who would like an orange?"

Still nobody spoke. Because nothing rhymes with 'orange'.

"Auah," said Mrs Sprout. "Everyone's infected."
Jasmine called out,
"But how can we make all this poetry **stop**?
If we don't discover a cure soon, I'll **POP!**"

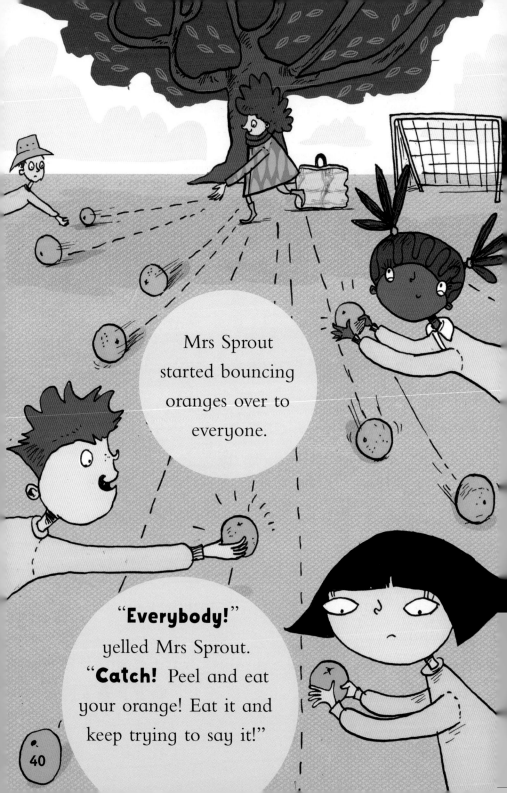

Mrs Sprout started bouncing oranges over to everyone.

"Everybody!" yelled Mrs Sprout. **"Catch!** Peel and eat your orange! Eat it and keep trying to say it!"

40

Everyone peeled their oranges quickly and took a bite. They made odd little grunts, trying to get the word 'orange' out. But their Rhyme-Slimed brains knew there was no rhyme in the world for 'orange'.

On her third bite, Jasmine felt something go *ping* in her head. "Orange!" she muttered. "Orange! **Orange! Orange!**

Orange!"

Suddenly, everyone was shouting "**Orange!**" Just 'orange'. Nothing else. "**Hooray!**" yelled Miss McCray. "Orange! And **purple!** Yes! Yes! We're **freeeee**! Well done, Class **2SB**!"

Silence fell as the children stared at her in horror. She was still rhyming! She coughed. "I mean, this has been quite an adventure, hasn't it?"

The children laughed and
shouted with delight. And not
one word was in rhyme.

"Just remember," said Mrs Sprout, as she zipped
up her purple bag. "Don't touch Poet's Pond goo
– you'll catch verse!"

Chapter Five

When Jasmine got home, she told Dad
and Anika all about it.

"So no more rhyming, Dad! **Whoopee!**"

"Good news. So what would you like for **tea**?"

Jasmine froze, staring at Dad. Was he rhyming? Then Anika said, "Curried chicken and rice for **me**!"

"Wait a minute," said Jasmine. "What are you **doing**?"

"I'll put the kettle on. Get it **brewing**," said Dad.

"I'll put the chicken on, get it **stewing**!" added Anika.

Jasmine sighed. "Who wants an orange?"

After reading activities

Quick quiz

See how fast you can answer these questions!
Look back at the story if you can't remember.

1) Where did Jasmine and the others get the
   rhyming infection from?

2) Who did Miss McCray call to come and help?

3) How did they get cured in the end?

Try this!

Try having a conversation in rhyme.
Ask someone to start it off by
saying something to you –
then reply with a sentence
that rhymes. Your rhymes
don't have to make sense!
How long can you keep it up?

Answers: 1) the goo in a pond; 2) Mrs Sprout;
3) Mrs Sprout made them try to say 'orange'.